TO CHRISTOPHER ROBINS HOUSE

POOHSTICKS BRIDGE

T POOHSTICKS BRIDGE

"I wish to pay tribute to the work of E.H. Shepard
which has been inspirational in the creation
of these new drawings."
Andrew Grey

First published in Great Britain 2004
By Egmont Books Limited
239 Kensington High Street, London W8 6SA
Illustrated by Andrew Grey
Based on the 'Winnie-the-Pooh' works
By A.A. Milne and E.H. Shepard
Text © The Trustees of the Pooh Properties
Illustrations © 2004 Disney Enterprises, Inc.
Designed by Clare Doughty
Edited by Catherine Shoolbred
All Rights Reserved.

1 3 5 7 9 10 8 6 4 2

ISBN 1 4052 1033 8

Printed in Singapore

Pooh Invents
A New Game

One day, Pooh was walking through the Forest trying to make up a piece of poetry about fir-cones. He picked one up, then this came into his head suddenly:

Here is a myst'ry
About a little fir-tree.
Owl says it's his tree,
And Kanga says it's her tree.

He had just reached a bridge and not looking where he was going, he tripped and the fir-cone jerked out of his paw into the river.

"Bother," said Pooh, as he lay down to watch the river. Suddenly, there was his fir-cone.

"That's funny," said Pooh. "I dropped it on the other side and it came out on this side! I wonder if it would do it again?" And he went back for some more fir-cones.

It did. It kept on doing it. Then he dropped one big one and one little one, and the big one came out first, which was what he had said it would do, and the little one came out last, which was what he had said it would do, so he had won twice.

And that was the beginning of the game called Poohsticks, that Pooh and his friends used to play with sticks instead of fir-cones, because they were easier to mark.

One day Pooh and Piglet and Rabbit and Roo were playing **Poohsticks**. They had dropped their sticks in when Rabbit said "Go!" and then hurried to the other side of the bridge to see whose stick would come out first.

"I can see mine!" cried Roo. "No, I can't, it's something else. Can you see yours, Pooh?"

"No," said Pooh.

"I expect my stick's stuck," said Roo.

"They always take longer than you think," said Rabbit.

"I can see yours, Piglet," said Pooh suddenly.
"It's coming over to my side."
Piglet got very excited because his was the
only one that had been seen, and that meant he
was winning.

"Are you *sure* it's mine?" he squeaked **excitedly**. "Yes, because it's grey. Here it comes! A very – big – grey – Oh, no, it isn't, it's Eeyore."

And out **floated** Eeyore.

"Eeyore, what *are* you doing there?" said Rabbit.
"I'll give you three guesses, Rabbit," said Eeyore.
"Digging holes in the ground? Wrong. Leaping from
branch to branch of a tree? Wrong. Waiting for
somebody to **help me out** of the river? Right."

"But, Eeyore," said Pooh, "what can we – I
mean, how shall we – do you think if we–"
"Yes," said Eeyore. "One of those would be
just the thing. Thank you, Pooh."

"I've got a sort of idea," said Pooh at last, "but I don't suppose it's a very good one."

"Go on, Pooh," said Rabbit.

"Well, if we threw stones into the river on *one* side of Eeyore, the stones would make waves, and the waves would wash him to the other side."

Pooh got a big stone and leant over the bridge.
"I'm not throwing it, I'm dropping it, Eeyore,"
he explained. "And then I can't miss – I mean I
can't hit you."
Pooh dropped his stone. There was a loud splash,
and Eeyore disappeared.

It was an anxious moment for the watchers on the bridge. Then something grey showed for a moment by the river bank. It slowly got bigger and bigger and at last it was Eeyore coming out. With a shout they rushed off the bridge.

"Well done, Pooh," said Rabbit kindly. "That was a good idea, hooshing Eeyore to the bank like that."

"*Hooshing* me?" said Eeyore in surprise. "Pooh dropped a large stone on me, and so as not to be struck heavily on the chest, I dived and swam to the bank."

"How did you fall in, Eeyore?" asked Rabbit.
"Somebody BOUNCED me. I was just thinking
by the side of the river, when I received a loud
BOUNCE," said Eeyore.
"But who did it?" asked Roo.
"I expect it was Tigger," said Piglet nervously.

There was a loud noise behind them, and
through the hedge came Tigger himself.

"Well done, Pooh," said Rabbit kindly. "That was a good idea, hooshing Eeyore to the bank like that."

"*Hooshing* me?" said Eeyore in surprise. "Pooh dropped a large stone on me, and so as not to be struck heavily on the chest, I dived and swam to the bank."

"That's what I call bouncing," said Eeyore. "Taking people by surprise."

"I didn't bounce, I coughed," said Tigger crossly. "Bouncy or coffy, it's all the same at the bottom of the river," said Eeyore.

Christopher Robin came down to the bridge and
saw all the animals there.

"It's like this, Christopher Robin," began Rabbit.
"Tigger–"

"All I did was I coughed," said Tigger.

"He bounced," said Eeyore.

"Well, I sort of boffed," said Tigger.

"Hush!" said Rabbit. "What does Christopher
Robin think about it all? That's the point."

"Well," said Christopher Robin, not quite sure
what it was all about. "*I* think we all ought to
play Poohsticks."

So they did. And Eeyore, who had never played it before, won more times than anybody else; and Roo fell in twice, the first time by accident and the second time on purpose, because he saw Kanga coming and knew he'd have to go to bed anyhow.

So then Rabbit said he'd go with them; and Tigger and Eeyore went off together. Christopher Robin and Pooh and Piglet were left on the bridge by themselves.

For a long time they looked at the river beneath them, saying nothing, and the river said nothing too, for it felt very quiet and peaceful on this summer afternoon.

"Tigger is all right, *really*," said Piglet lazily.
"Of course he is," said Christopher Robin.
"Everybody is *really*," said Pooh. "That's what
I think, but I don't suppose I'm right."
"Of course you are," said Christopher Robin.

POOH BEARS HOUSE

GOOD PLACE FOR PINE CONES

TO PIGLETS HOUSE

THIS STORY TOOK PLAC